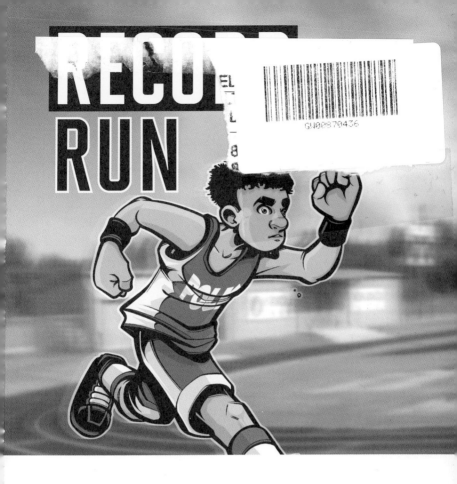

# RECORD RUN

## Eric Stevens

### illustrated by Sean Tiffany

**Librarian Reviewer**
Chris Kreie, Media Specialist

**Reading Consultant**

**www.raintreepublishers.co.uk**
Visit our website to find out
more information about
Raintree books.

**To order:**
☎ Phone 0845 6044371
🖨 Fax +44 (0) 1865 312263
✉ Email myorders@capstonepub.co.uk

Customers from outside the UK please telephone +44 1865 312262

Raintree is an imprint of Capstone Global Library Limited, a company
incorporated in England and Wales having its registered office at 7 Pilgrim
Street, London, EC4V 6LB – Registered company number: 6695582

"Raintree" is a registered trademark of Pearson Education Limited,
under licence to Capstone Global Library Limited

Edited in the UK by Laura Knowles
Art Director: Heather Kindseth
Graphic Designer: Carla Zetina-Yglesias
Originated by Capstone Global Library
Printed and bound in China by Leo Paper Products Ltd

ISBN 978 1 406213 79 9 (hardback)
14 13 12 11 10
10 9 8 7 6 5 4 3 2 1

ISBN 978 1 406214 00 0 (paperback)
14 13 12 11 10
10 9 8 7 6 5 4 3 2 1

**British Library Cataloguing in Publication Data**
Stevens, Eric, 1974-
Record run. -- (Sport stories)
813.6-dc22
A full catalogue record for this book is available from the British Library.

# CONTENTS

# CHAPTER 1

# THE TWO-POINTER

Harry Miller and Jake Bell were laughing. The Year 7 kids were crouched together in a climbing frame at a park near Puckley Community School.

The climbing frame they were hiding in was built to look like a pirate ship. At the top was a wood cabin.

From inside the cabin, Jake and Harry could see the whole park, but no one could see them.

"Okay, Jake," Harry said, still laughing. "That's three for you, and two for me."

"You bet it is," Jake replied. "Looks like I'll win again."

A big pile of water balloons was next to the boys. Harry reached out and picked one up.

"You only have one throw left," Jake said. "Even if you get someone soaking wet, you can only tie the score."

Harry thought for a second. "What if I score a two-pointer?" he asked.

Jake laughed and shook his head. "You must be nuts," he said. "You have to soak someone from Year 9 to get two points. Are you really that crazy?"

Harry smiled. "I'll do whatever it takes to win," he said.

Jake shrugged. "We'll see," he replied. "We can't wait all day for someone from Year 9 to walk past."

Harry slowly got to his knees and peeked through the window. He turned his head to look carefully over the whole park, trying to spot someone to throw the next water balloon at.

"There," Harry said, pointing.

Jake got up and looked through the window. "Where?" he asked.

Harry was pointing towards the edge of the park. Two boys from their school, both from Year 9, were leaning against the fence.

"Look at them," Harry said. "They look like they're half asleep. They'll never know it was me."

Jake laughed. "Maybe," he said. "But they're pretty far off. I bet you can't even reach them with a water balloon from here."

"Who said I have to throw it from here?" Harry said.

"What are you going to do, walk right up to them?" Jake replied.

"If that's what it takes to win!" Harry said. He tossed the water balloon lightly in his hand. "So, are you going to come with me?"

Jake shook his head. "No way, mate," he said. "If you hit one of them, you win. But I'm staying right here where it's safe."

Harry shrugged. "Suit yourself," he said. Then he climbed down the ladder out of the cabin.

Harry took a few cautious steps towards the two Year 9 boys. He stopped behind a tree when he thought he was close enough.

Harry glanced back at the pirate ship cabin. He could see Jake's face peeking through the window.

"Well, here goes nothing," Harry muttered to himself. Then he stepped out from behind the tree.

The two boys were facing the other way and still seemed half asleep. Harry pulled back his arm. With all his might, he heaved the water balloon towards the two older boys.

The water balloon hit one of them right in the back and exploded. It sent a flood of water all over the boy.

Right away, Harry stepped back behind the tree to hide. If he started running, the boys would easily spot him.

"Please, don't let them see me!" he whispered to himself.

"Hey!" a voice shouted. "Who threw that water balloon at me? You better come out now if you know what's good for you!"

Harry stayed completely still and silent. He listened carefully.

"I think I saw someone run behind that tree," another voice replied. "I bet it was him!"

"Oh yeah?" said the first voice again. "Let's go and find out."

"Uh-oh," Harry whispered. He decided it was time to start running.

"Get him!" the first voice said again.

Harry glanced over his shoulder as he ran. One of the boys — the dry one — wasn't very fast. After a few seconds of running, he just stopped and caught his breath.

But the boy Harry had hit with the balloon was still chasing him. And he looked really mad!

# CHAPTER 2

# THE CHASE

Harry ran as fast he could. "At least this means I beat Jake," he thought as he ran. "I got more water-balloon points than he did."

He managed to smile as he picked up speed. Harry didn't really know the Year 9 boy he'd hit. He had seen him around school, but otherwise he didn't know anything about him.

"It's not like he's going to beat me up or anything," Harry thought.

Still, Harry didn't want to get caught. It wouldn't feel like a real victory if he got caught. And Jake would definitely make fun of him.

Harry glanced over his shoulder again. The kid was catching up. Harry tried to run a bit faster.

Soon he reached the north end of the park. But suddenly he realized something. He hadn't been paying attention to where he was going.

He wasn't thinking as he ran, and he forgot the north end of the park didn't have a gate. Harry was running at full speed, right at a metre-high fence!

"Uh-oh," he muttered to himself. "Guess I have no choice, though. I'm going to have to jump it."

Just before he ran smack into the fence, Harry took an extra deep breath. Then he jumped as far and high as he could. He cleared the fence so easily, he even surprised himself.

"Stop!" the boy behind him called.

Harry kept running. He was sure the older boy would stop at the fence. When Harry glanced behind him, though, he saw the older boy glide effortlessly over the fence.

"Whoa," Harry said as he ran on. He was starting to get tired now.

After a few more steps, he felt something tug on his collar. He was pulled to a stop.

"Gotcha!" the older boy said with a huff.

Harry was caught!

# CHAPTER 3

# CAUGHT

"Get your hands off me!" Harry said. He spun around and managed to get his shirt out of the older boy's hand.

"Take it easy," the boy replied. "I'm not going to hurt you."

"I almost got away," Harry said.

"Yeah, I noticed," the older boy replied. "Why did you throw that water balloon at me? I don't even know you."

Harry shrugged. "It's a game I play with my friend," he said. "We get a point for each kid we hit with a balloon. But we get two points if we hit someone from Year 9."

"I see," the older boy said. "So you got two points for me?"

Harry smiled. "That's right," he said. "In fact, I beat Jake by a point thanks to that hit."

"Well, at least I was the winning attack," the older boy replied. "Truth is, I was going to drag you by the collar to the fountain and drench you."

"So what's stopping you?" Harry asked, frowning. "You caught me."

The older boy laughed. "To be honest, I didn't think you'd put up such a good chase," he said.

"What do you mean?" Harry asked.

"You're fast," the boy replied. "And I can't believe how easily you got over that fence. It was pretty amazing."

Harry shrugged again. "It was easy," he said. "So you're not going to soak me?

The other boy shook his head. Then he looked at Harry and frowned. "What's your name?" he asked.

"Harry Miller," Harry replied.

The older boy said, "Harry Miller, I'm Paul Dobson. And I won't soak you on one condition."

Harry squinted at Paul. "What's that?" he asked.

"After a run like that, what else?" Paul said. "You have to join the Puckley Community School running team."

"The running team?" Harry said. "You must be kidding. I'm only in Year 7. No one makes it onto a sports team in Year 7."

"Don't worry about that," Paul said. "I'm the team captain. When I tell Mr Andrews how fast you are, he'll let you on the team. I have no doubt about it."

Harry looked at his feet. "Can I think about it?" he said, looking up.

"Sure," Paul said. "Let me know tomorrow. But my friends and I will be ready with about a hundred water balloons. And we'll be right outside the school at three tomorrow if I don't hear from you before then."

Harry nodded. "Okay, I get it," he said. "You'll hear from me before then."

# CHAPTER 4

# LUNCH

The next day at lunch, Harry plonked his tray down next to Jake's on the table.

"This is so lame," Harry said. Angrily, he sat down in the plastic chair.

"What is?" Jake asked. "It's pizza day. Nothing lame about pizza." Jake stuffed a slice of pizza into his mouth and savoured it slowly.

"Not the pizza," Harry replied. "I mean the running team thing."

Jake nodded and swallowed his mouthful. "Oh, right," he said. "That. Well, so join the team. It's not like you have to try hard once you're on the team or anything."

"What do you mean? Do you think I should agree to join?" Harry asked. "And then show up to practices, but not make any effort?"

Jake nodded. He sipped his juice. "Why not?," he said. "Paul just said you have to join, right? You don't have to win a medal. Or break all the school records or anything."

Harry nodded slowly. "That's true," he said. He glanced at the clock. Then he went on, "I suppose I should go and find Paul. I'll be in lessons the rest of the day. Then, at three, he's going to drench us if I don't find him first."

"Us?" Jake repeated. He gasped. "What do you mean? How did I get involved in this?"

Harry got out of his seat. He replied, "Well, we usually leave school together. And if that happens, I have a feeling you'll be in the line of fire."

"In that case, good luck, mate," Jake said. He took another big bite of pizza. "I'm sure you'll look great in your running kit!"

Jake laughed as Harry walked off to find Paul. Harry tried not to let it get to him.

* * *

Harry was pretty sure where he'd find Paul. Most of the sporty kids from Year 9 ate lunch in the courtyard. He'd look there first.

Harry pushed open the courtyard doors and stepped into the sun.

He squinted for a minute and shaded his eyes. Looking back and forth, he scanned the crowd of kids eating at the plastic picnic tables.

"Hey, Harry!" someone called out. "You looking for me?"

Harry turned and spotted Paul waving at him. He was sitting with five other kids, including two girls. Harry didn't know any of their names.

Harry waved back and started walking over. At the same time, Paul jumped up. He jogged towards Harry. The other kids at the table laughed a little when they saw Harry.

"So, have you made up your mind?" Paul asked. "You ready to be our next running star or what?"

Harry thought for a minute longer.

"Do I really want to give up my afternoons and join the running team?" he thought. "Or should I just take my soaking and get on with my life?"

Harry frowned, thinking about it. "Then again," he thought, "I don't think I want every kid in the team to spend the rest of the year soaking me with water balloons every time they see me."

"I guess I've made up my mind," Harry finally said. "I'll join the school running team."

"Excellent!" Paul said. He put out his hand for a high five.

Harry threw up his hands. "I can't promise I'm going to be a running star, you know," he said. "I'll be the youngest on the team."

Paul smiled and shook his head. "No worries," he said. "I've seen you run. Just show up at the track today at four, okay? I'll talk to Mr Andrews."

Harry nodded. "Okay, I'll be there then," he said.

"If I have to," he added to himself.

# CHAPTER 5

# FIRST PRACTICE

A few minutes before four o'clock, Jake and Harry stood at the back door of the school. They could see the running track at the far end of the field. Lots of kids were standing around in red and gold uniforms. Most of them were stretching or jogging in place.

"Those are some silly-looking uniforms," Jake said. He shook his head slowly. "I wouldn't be caught dead in one of those."

Harry looked down at his own uniform. Paul had given it to him. "Well, you don't have to join the team," Harry replied, "so bog off."

"Hope it's not too bad," Jake said. "Have fun." He popped some gum into his mouth and walked off.

"Yeah, I'm sure I will," Harry replied under his breath. Then he started jogging across the field towards the track.

"Here he comes, Mr Andrews," Paul was saying as Harry jogged up. "That's Harry Miller. He's the one I told you about."

Harry stopped in front of Paul and the coach. "Hi," he said nervously.

"Okay, Miller," Mr Andrews said. "You don't look so tough to me. Paul says you're fast."

Harry shrugged. "Yeah, I suppose I'm pretty fast," he said.

"He's definitely fast, Mr Andrews," Paul added. "I saw this kid run 400 metres — with hurdles — in under a minute the other day."

The coach raised his eyebrows. "Under a minute?" he repeated, surprised. "That would be impressive."

The coach looked at Harry again. "Okay, son," Mr Andrews said. "I'll give you a shot, if Paul says you're up to it. I'll bring a uniform for you tomorrow. For today, just pay attention and do your best."

With that, the coach walked off. He stood in the centre of the track and blew his whistle. All the team members stopped their warm-ups and gathered around.

Paul headed towards the group. Harry grabbed Paul by the wrist to stop him. "Hey, what was that all about?" Harry asked.

"What do you mean?" Paul replied.

"That stuff about 400 metres and hurdles," Harry explained. "I don't even know what that means! There's no way you ever saw me run it."

Paul laughed. "You'll find out what it means pretty soon," he said. "But I was talking about yesterday, Harry. That chase you led me on was about 400 metres. And you cleared that fence like it was nothing! Just like a hurdler. You're a natural!"

Paul laughed again. Then he headed over to the coach with the other team members.

Harry stood where he was for a moment. As he looked at the track team, he thought, "Maybe I will be good at this running stuff after all."

# CHAPTER 6

# NOT GOOD ENOUGH

"Okay, Miller," Mr Andrews said. "Let's talk."

The other runners had already split off into groups after a short talk from the coach. But Harry hadn't been sure which group he was supposed to join.

"Dobson says you're a 400 man," the coach said.

"I guess so," Harry replied.

"Okay then," the coach went on. He glanced at his clipboard. Then he pointed at a group of guys. "Head over there, with group B. They'll be running single lap drills."

"Single lap drills. Okay," Harry said.

"One lap is 400 metres, Miller," the coach replied. "You have run a lap before, right?"

"Of course I have," Harry replied. "No problem."

The coach nodded. "Off you go," he said. Then he walked away to watch the team practise.

Harry jogged over to group B and joined them. There were about ten other boys getting ready to run the single lap drills.

"Hey, new kid," one of the runners said. "Are you going to run 400s?"

Harry nodded. "I guess so," he said.

"Okay then," the other boy said. "Line up. You can run with the first crew. We'll keep your time. Go on the whistle."

"Okay," Harry replied. He walked over to the other boys at the start line and stood with them.

"On your marks!" shouted the boy who had shown Harry where to go. "Get set!"

The other boys on the start line crouched down a little. Harry tried to copy them.

An instant later, the whistle blew. The runners shot off the line. Harry was a little slow to start, but he got up to speed pretty quickly.

Harry did his best to stay with the other runners. He watched them and copied their running style.

"This is a long run," he thought. "There's no way Paul chased me that far yesterday."

Just looking at how big the track was made him feel totally exhausted. He felt himself slowing down. With every step he took, he heard his feet slapping the weird rubbery pavement of the track.

It seemed like forever before he reached the finish line. He managed to beat a few of the other runners he'd started with.

"One minute, fifteen seconds," the boy at the finish called as Harry ran by. Mr Andrews was waiting at the finish line too.

"Not too bad, Miller," the coach said. "You're definitely a strong runner, especially for someone in Year 7."

"Thanks, Mr Andrews," Harry replied, smiling. He was feeling pretty proud.

"Still, a minute fifteen isn't exactly under a minute," Mr Andrews added. "Paul said you could run the 400 in less than sixty seconds. You're not going to make a liar out of my team captain, are you?"

Harry swallowed. "Um, no, Mr Andrews," he said. "I promise."

"All right then," the coach replied. Then he walked off to check on the boys doing high jumps.

Suddenly someone grabbed Harry's shoulder.

"Hey!" Harry said, spinning around. It was Paul.

"What was that all about, man?" Paul asked.

"What? What are you talking about?" Harry said.

"I told him you were fast," Paul replied. "You didn't really put on the speed out there today, did you?"

Harry shrugged. "I don't know," he said.

Paul took a deep breath and sighed. "Well," he said, "I know you're faster than that. You were probably just nervous. You'll do better next time."

With that, Paul walked off.

"What does he know?" Harry thought. "I never said I could run anyway."

# CHAPTER 7

# BORING

That Saturday, Jake sat at Harry's computer. "This game is amazing," Jake said. A loud, wicked laugh came from the computer speakers.

"What happened?" Harry asked.

"Ah, he beat me again," Jake said.

"You'll figure it out," Harry said. "Just try again." Harry lay down on his bed and started flipping through a new comic book.

"Hey, how's the running going, anyway?" Jake asked. "Did you go to practice every day this week?"

Harry nodded, but he didn't look up from the comic he was reading. "Yeah, I went," he said. "It's pretty boring, though."

"Really?" Jake asked, surprised. "Aren't you the next big running star yet?"

Harry shrugged. "No way," he said. "Besides, like I said, it's boring. All you do is run in a circle about a hundred times."

"Yeah, that does sound boring," Jake said. "I mean, if you're not being chased, why run as hard as you can? You might as well take it easy."

Suddenly Jake pounded wildly at the keyboard of Harry's computer.

"Oi, be careful with my keyboard!" Harry said, getting up.

"Sorry," Jake said. "I almost won that time."

Harry shook his head. "There's no game you can play as well as I can, is there?" he asked with a chuckle.

Jake leaned forwards again. "That sounds like a challenge to me!" he said. He started up the game again.

Harry just laughed and went back to reading his comic.

# CHAPTER 8

# OLD TRICKS

After the weekend, Harry wasn't looking forward to running practice. At three o'clock on Monday afternoon, he and Jake headed through the rear exit of Puckley School.

Harry stopped and looked at the track across the field. "Ugh," he said. "Another day of running practice." He shook his head. "I am not looking forward to this," he added.

"Don't you want to go?" Jake asked.

Harry shrugged. "Not really," he replied. "I think I'll skip it, in fact. Let's go to the park for a few minutes."

"And do what?" Jake said. "I'm all out of water balloons."

Harry smiled. "I've got about a hundred in my bag," he said. "We're all set."

"Nice," Jake replied. The two headed across the grass towards the park.

* * *

Forty-five minutes later, Harry spotted Paul running through the park, carrying his track uniform.

"He must have forgotten that at home," Harry told Jake. They were sitting in the pirate ship climbing frame, hidden from view. "He's pretty late for practice," Harry went on. "He's going to be in huge trouble."

"Hit him with a balloon!" Jake suggested.

Harry laughed, a little too loudly. Paul stopped and looked up.

At that moment, Harry tossed a water balloon right at Paul. He missed, but the water balloon exploded on the ground near Paul's feet. It splashed his trainers.

Paul looked up at the pirate ship climbing frame again. "Harry!" he called out. "Come down from there."

Harry peeked over the wall of the ship's cabin. "What's up?" he said with a laugh.

"It's almost four," Paul replied. "Aren't you going to practice?"

Harry shrugged. "Nah," he said. "I don't think so. It's really boring. Anyway, my times haven't been very good. I don't think Mr Andrews will miss me."

Paul was about to start arguing, but Harry raised his arm and whipped another water balloon over the wall.

It shot right past Paul and hit a sixth form boy who was walking through the park. It splattered water all over the boy's trousers.

"Sixth former!" Harry whispered. "That's got to be at least four or five points."

"Hey!" the sixth former shouted. He turned and eyed Paul. "Did you throw that balloon at me?" the sixth form boy asked.

Paul shook his head. "No way. Wasn't me!" he insisted. Harry and Jake laughed. Paul looked up at the pirate ship.

The sixth former looked up at the pirate ship cabin too.

"Who's up there?" the high school boy asked loudly.

"Uh-oh," Jake and Harry said together.

The sixth form boy started running towards them.

"You better run, Harry," Paul said, looking up the ladder.

"Oh, man," Harry said. He climbed down the ladder as fast as he could. "Here we go again!"

Harry took off like a shot. He ran right at the fence at the far end of the park. With ease, he leapt over the fence.

The sixth form boy was much older and bigger than Harry. Harry thought the older boy would easily be able to clear the fence too.

But in mid-air, one of the older boy's trainers caught on the top of the fence and he tumbled onto the grass. He quickly got up and brushed himself off, but by then Harry was out of sight.

Paul followed close behind and soon caught up to Harry. "Harry," he called out. "Come to practice."

"Why?" Harry replied. "I'm no good. The coach said himself that my time on the 400 wasn't good enough. And I'd rather go home and play computer games or hang out at the park with Jake."

"I know you can run like a record breaker," Paul replied. "That chase was more proof! Just give it one more chance."

# CHAPTER 9

# TO WIN

Harry stood, catching his breath for a moment. He glanced over Paul's shoulder to make sure the sixth form boy wasn't chasing him anymore.

The coast was clear.

"I don't know, Paul," Harry said. "I need a reason to run. It's like my friend Jake said. If I'm not being chased, what's the point in running?"

Paul nodded. "So you need a good reason," he said. "Well, why do you do anything?"

"What do you mean?" Harry asked.

Paul pointed at the pirate ship climbing frame. "Why do you throw water balloons?" he asked.

Harry shrugged. "It's fun," he said. "Besides, I always get more points than Jake." He smiled.

"What about those computer games?" Paul asked. "What's your reason for that?"

"Finishing them," Harry replied. "Once I finish a game a couple of times, I don't usually play it anymore."

"You can finish a computer game?" Paul asked.

"Of course," Harry answered. "That's how you win."

"So nothing is fun for you," Paul said, "unless you can win? You really do love to compete."

Harry thought for a second. "I suppose so," he replied.

Paul glanced at his watch. "We need to get to practice," he said. "But I have two things you should think about. Meets and personal bests."

"What do you mean?" Harry said. He followed Paul towards the boys' locker room.

"Competition!" Paul said. "It's what you thrive on!"

Harry thought about that. "Okay," he said slowly.

"Just for today," Paul added quickly, "I'm going to run the 400 drills with you."

"Why?" Harry asked. "You're a miler, aren't you?"

"Just for today," Paul repeated. "I have an idea."

# CHAPTER 10

# PERSONAL BEST

Harry and Paul were only a few minutes late to practice. They jogged over to the 400 group.

"Paul, you're in the wrong group," one of the 400-metre runners said. "Shouldn't you be training with the other milers?"

"I'm training with you guys for today," Paul replied.

The others glanced at each other. "Whatever you say," one of them said.

"If it's all right with you guys," Paul added, "the first drill will be just me and Harry with a full lap."

The others said that was okay. Harry and Paul stepped up to the start line.

"Harry, you take the outside lane," Paul said. "I'll take the inside behind you."

"You want me to start ahead of you?" Harry asked. "That's not fair."

"No," Paul replied. "The outside lane always starts a metre or so ahead to make up for the curve in the track. If you're on the outside, you have to run a little bit further to make it around the curve than the person on the inside does."

"Oh, I get it," Harry said.

"Besides," Paul added, "this way I can chase you."

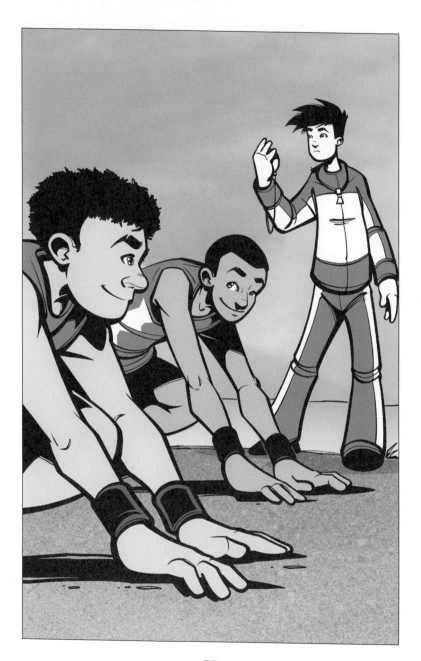

Harry took off at the whistle. He heard Paul's footsteps close behind him.

"Better not let me catch you," Paul taunted.

Harry picked up his speed a little. He could tell Paul was falling further behind. Harry smiled as he rounded the last curve.

The finish line was in sight.

Harry glanced over his shoulder. He could see that Paul was about five metres behind him. Harry was easily going to win!

Harry stepped over the finish line. Paul crossed the line a few seconds later. Mr Andrews was right there with his clipboard. As Harry stopped to catch his breath, he listened for his time.

"One minute, two seconds," called out the boy with the stopwatch.

Harry slowed to a walk and strolled back towards the coach. Paul asked, "How did I do?"

The timer called out, "One minute and five seconds."

"Nice job, Harry," the coach said. "That's your personal best time."

"Thanks, Mr Andrews," Harry replied.

Mr Andrews looked at Paul. "I guess he is as good as you say he is," the coach said. "I bet he'll be able to run the 400 in a minute before we know it. Might get him under a minute yet."

Mr Andrews winked at Harry. Then he walked off to check on the sprinters.

"Well done, Harry," Paul said. "I knew you just needed some motivation."

"Thanks," Harry replied. "But you can't chase me in every race!"

"Now you can chase yourself," Paul said.

"Chase myself?" Harry asked, confused. "What are you talking about?"

"Don't you get it?" Paul said. "Last week, your best time was a minute and eleven seconds, right?"

"Right," Harry said.

"Today, you ran one minute and two seconds," Paul went on. "If you keep at it, you can shave another couple of seconds off that score."

"You mean get an even better time?" Harry said.

"Right," said Paul.

"So my only competition," Harry concluded, "is myself."

"The best competition there is," Paul added.

Harry nodded. "I can do that," he said. "I'm the only competition I need!"

## ABOUT THE AUTHOR

Eric Stevens is studying to become an English teacher. Some of his favourite things include pizza, playing computer games, watching cooking programmes on TV, riding his bike, and trying new restaurants. One of his least favourite things is olives.

## ABOUT THE ILLUSTRATOR

When Sean Tiffany was growing up, he lived on a small island. Every day, he had to take a boat to get to school. When Sean isn't working on his art, he works on a multimedia project called "OilCan Drive", which combines music and art. He has a pet cactus named Jim.

# GLOSSARY

**cautious** if you are cautious, you try to avoid mistakes and danger

**drench** to make something completely wet

**effortlessly** without trying

**exhausted** very tired

**heaved** threw

**impressive** thought highly of by others

**natural** person who is good at something because of a special talent or ability

**squad** a team

**victory** a win in a contest or battle

# MORE ABOUT
## FAMOUS RUNNERS

Between 1979 and 1996, **Carl Lewis** won 10 Olympic medals, including 9 gold medals. He also won 10 World Championship medals, including 8 gold medals. The International Olympic Committee awarded him the Sportsman of the Century honour, and *Sports Illustrated* named him Olympian of the Century. Lewis is most famous for his sprinting, both in individual events and as a member of a relay team.

**Archie Hahn** was the author of the book *How to Sprint*. Born in 1880, Hahn was one of the best sprinters of the first half of the 20th century. In the 1904 Olympics, held in St. Louis, Missouri, Hahn won three gold medals, in the 60 metre race, the 100 metre race, and the 200 metre race. Two years later, at a special Olympics known as the Intercalated Games, Hahn won the gold medal in the 100 metre race. He died in 1955.

**Michael Johnson**, a sprinter, won 4 Olympic gold medals and 9 world championships. He holds the world record for the 400 metre race and the 4 x 400 metre relay. One of the things Johnson is most famous for is his unique running style. While most runners take long strides and lift their legs, Johnson takes very short steps and keeps his body very upright.

**Usain Bolt** is a young sprinter from Jamaica. At the 2008 Olympic Games in Beijing, at the age of 21, Bolt broke the world records for both the 100 metre race (9.69 seconds) and the 200 metre race (19.30 seconds), as well as the 4 x 100 metre relay (37.10 seconds). Bolt is the only person ever to have set world records in all three events at a single Olympic Games. At the World Athletics Championships in 2009, Bolt broke his own world record, winning the 100 metres in 9.58 seconds. He has been nicknamed "Lightning Bolt" because of his amazing speed.

# DISCUSSION QUESTIONS

1. Why did Harry join the running team? What else could he have done to keep Paul from being mad at him?

2. Harry says that kids his age never make the sports teams. What happens at your school? Do kids your age play sports? What sports do they play?

3. Harry and his best friend made up the water balloon game. What games do you play with your friends?

# WRITING PROMPTS

1. At the beginning of this book, Harry spends a lot of time with his best friend. Write about your best friend.

2. Harry doesn't think he'll be good at being in the running team. Write about a time you tried something you weren't sure you'd be good at. What did you try? What happened?

3. Harry hits Paul with a water balloon. What if he had hit someone else? Write a story in which Harry hits someone else with the water balloon. How would things be different?

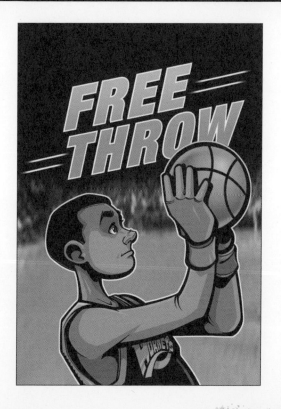

Theo is the tallest kid on his basketball team, so his coach decides to have him play centre instead of Jason. Theo thinks this is a lucky break, until Jason takes revenge. Will he ever be able to make a free thow with Jason breathing down his neck?

Matt's chances of making the racing team are threatened when Alex moves into town. Alex is a cheat, and as mean as they come out on the racetrack. Matt insists on riding by the rules. Unless somebody stops Alex cheating, Matt wont make the team...

# FIND OUT MORE

**BOOKS**

*Inside Sport: Athletics*, Clive Gifford (Wayland, 2010)

*Sporting Skills: Athletics*, Clive Gifford (Wayland, 2008)

*Starting Sport: Athletics*, Rebecca Hunter (Franklin Watts, 2009)

*Track Athletics*, Jason Page (ticktock Media, 2008)

*Training to Succeed: Track Athletics*, Rita Storey (Franklin Watts, 2009)